AMY KROUSE ROSENTHAL & TOM LICHTENHELD

HarperCollins*Publishers*

the OK book

Hi, how are you?
I'm OK.

I like to try a lot of different things.

I'm not great at all of them,
but I enjoy them just the same.

I'm an OK skipper.

I'm an OK climber.

I'm an OK marshmallow roaster.

I'm an OK tightrope walker.

I'm an OK left fielder.

I'm an OK right fielder.

I'm an OK diver.

I'm an OK hider.

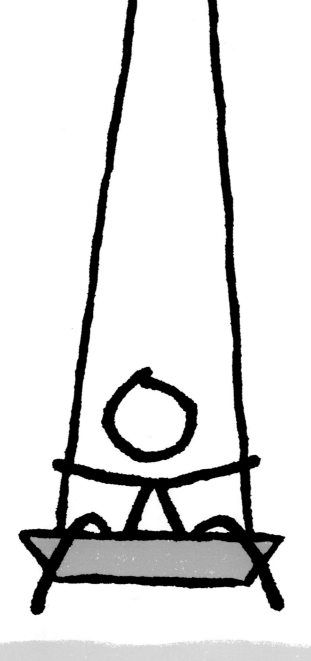

I'm an OK pumper.

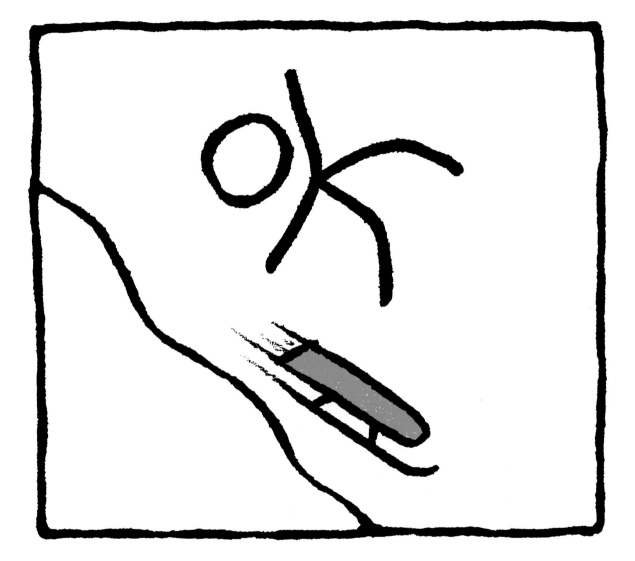

I'm an OK sledder.

I'm an OK kite flyer.

I'm an OK tug-of-war-er.

I'm an OK sharer.

I'm an OK headstander.

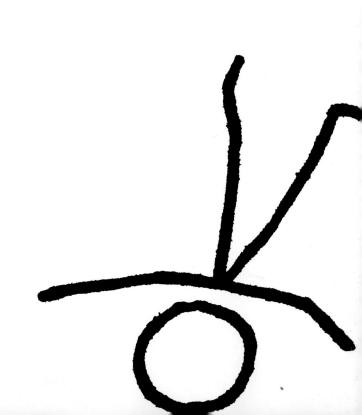

I'm an OK pancake flipper.

I'm an OK fisher.

I'm an OK swimmer.

I'm an OK lightning bug catcher.

One day, I'll grow up to be really excellent at something.

I don't know what it is yet...

...but I sure am having fun figuring it out.

The end.

For information address HarperCollins Children's Books, a division of HarperCollins
Publishers, 195 Broadway, New York, NY 10007.
www.harpercollinschildrens.com

Library of Congress Cataloging-in-Publication Data is available.
ISBN-10: 0-06-115255-2 (trade bdg.) — ISBN-13: 978-0-06-115255-9 (trade bdg.)
ISBN-10: 0-06-115256-0 (lib. bdg.) — ISBN-13: 978-0-06-115256-6 (lib. bdg.)

Typography by Jeanne L. Hogle
19 20 21 SCP 20 19 18
❖
First Edition

kook productions
amy krouse rosenthal & tom lichtenheld

Or is it just the beginning?